MEET THE WILD PACK

¡ Cuy Brito delicioso! .

Luigi Celin

JUICY JACK adventures

MEET THE WILD PACK

by Leigh Carrasco

illustrations by Angela Mia De la Vega

Text copyright © 2014 Leigh Carrasco
Illustrations copyright © 2014 Angela Mia De la Vega

JUICY JACK ADVENTURES: Meet The Wild Pack
ISBN 978-0-9904023-0-5 (paperback)

Text by Leigh Carrasco,
Illustrations by Angela Mia De la Vega
Published by Womeldorf Press

First Edition – 2014 / Edited by Chuck Sambuchino,
Book Design by Kari Zeigler

Printed in August 2014 in the
United States of America by

1124 Oneida Valley Road
Chicora, PA 16025
www.mechlingbooks.com

For my loving husband and amazing sons.
-L.C.

•●•

For my endlessly loving parents,
Dr. John and Kathleen Smith.
-A.M.D.

Contents

Chapter 1 1

Chapter 2 15

Chapter 3 25

Chapter 4 37

Chapter 5 51

Chapter 6 61

Chapter 7 73

Chapter 8 83

Chapter 9 91

Chapter 10 101

Chapter 11 113

Spanish-English Word Glossary 121

Label the Vegetables 124

Andean Customs 127

CHAPTER 1

Please Don't Leave Me

On most days, Jack behaved like a good little guinea pig - for instance, when he sat on BT's shoulder or when he was asleep. On this particular afternoon, Jack was definitely not on his human's shoulder and definitely not asleep.

"Jack . . . Jack," said BT. "Where's my Beast of the East?"

Jack usually rushed from wherever he was hiding at the sound of BT's call, but not today. He had lip-smacking food on his mind. Not even the thud of BT's backpack hitting the kitchen floor made Jack flinch.

There was nothing like a juicy piece of celery - well, maybe a slice of apple or sprig of parsley. Mother was a deliciously sloppy cook. If only he could get just one piece of anything!

"BT, please keep it down! I'm on hold with the airline," called Mother. She tossed a crusty pan into the sink and pulled a clean one from the cabinet. "Yes, yes, I'm still here. That's correct, from Knoxville, tomorrow. Yes, Jack's our pet."

Jack peeked around the recycle bin to see Mother put her hand over the telephone and plant a kiss on BT's head. "I think Jack's in the living room again," she said. "You shouldn't have taught him to open his cage."

Jack chuckled and pushed his belly aside to crouch like a jaguar. His muscles got in the way at times like this. He crept forward, humming his favorite spy tune.

"Da, da, da ... da, sneak, sneak.
"Da, da, da ... da, squeak, squeak."

He licked his lips and stifled a squeal. It was difficult for a guinea pig not to squeal. The aroma of chopped vegetables was tantalizing.

"Squeak!" Jack cupped his paws over his mouth.

"Beast of the East, come out! We have to get ready for the trip. Where's my Roughest, Toughest, Orange, Mohawkiest, Guinea Beast?"

Jack slinked closer and closer to the celery. Wait a minute, did BT say, "we"?

"Yikes!" Jack darted back, away from Mother's foot and flattened himself against the recycle bin just in time to feel the cool metal hum vibrate through his body as Mother's foot kicked it. Jack was knocked over but immediately sprang back into position, hoping Mother hadn't seen him. She would put him back in his cage if she found him.

How could she not see Jack, she was standing just on the other side? Jack's hair stood on end making him look more like a porcupine than a guinea pig. He held his breath and waited. The pounding of his heart got louder and louder. Surely Mother heard it, too.

But she didn't.

What was she doing? Jack scratched his furry chin and stretched his neck to make sure the celery was still on the floor. Maybe Mother wouldn't see him if he ran quickly. He wiped his bristly brow and mentally prepared to go full-out commando. . . .

Beep! Beep! Beep!

Or, even better, get a little help from the kitchen timer.

Mother rushed to the stove to avoid yet another burned dinner. Jack lunged in, snatched the chunk of celery with his teeth, and was gone in a flash. He dashed through the living room, zigged into the hallway, zagged around a suitcase, jumped over a pile of building blocks and came to a halt in front of the bedroom mirror.

He winked at himself and shook his orange mohawk.

"I'm Jack Attack, Beast of the East!" Jack smirked then burrowed under dirty clothes to gobble his prize.

"Jack. Jack!" called out BT.

Jack popped the last bite into his mouth then peeked out from his secret hiding spot behind the laundry basket. He waited for BT to turn away then scurried under the bed and out the other side.

"Come here, my little Jack Attack. I have a radish for you," teased BT.

BT sat down and pulled Jack onto his lap to stroke the stiff orange and white cowlicks that lined Jack's back. His other hand busied itself pulling slime from his nose. Jack watched BT examine the booger closely then smear it onto his big toe. Jack squealed and choked on the radish. That booger would be dry and crusty just in time for a quick bedtime snack. That's my Booger Toe!

(Jack never had understood why mother didn't use BT's full name.)

BT put Jack on the floor to finish his radish. Jack nibbled and watched his human rush around the room putting clothes, books and video games into a suitcase. Usually, BT sat at his desk after school. That was boring, but today was different, at least until Mother called BT to the kitchen. Jack peaked around the corner and saw BT sit down at the table. It was dinner-time so he went to his cage and ate a few strands of Timothy Hay.

After dinner, BT lay in his beanbag with Jack stretched across his shoulder. They always watched television together. That was how Jack learned English and realized how smart he was. He wished he could speak to humans too, but no matter how hard he tried, the only sounds to escape his mouth were squeaks and squeals. One time, Jack tried speaking louder, thinking that would make it easier for his humans to understand him.

It didn't.

Tonight was the final part in a series about Peru - a whole different country. Last night Jack learned that jaguars were honored for their courage and cleverness. The program left Jack certain that jaguars were good role models for him. A man called an archeologist found a small

gold statue of a jaguar in a tomb. That was pretty cool. Jack wished he could ask BT if any gold guinea pigs had ever been found.

Tonight's show talked about the hidden treasures of the Inca. Jack already knew that the first Inca, born hundreds of years ago, was believed to be the son of the sun. Was that even possible? BT did an oral report on him last year. Jack and Mother listened to him practice his presentation, over and over. Jack was very interested in finding treasure so he watched the television program closely. Maybe there was a hidden treasure somewhere in their house?

Mother poked her head into the room. "Benjamin, you know you're not allowed to watch more than an hour a day during the school week."

"Today was the last day of school. It's officially summer vacation!" said BT.

Mother softened her tone. "Well, don't fall asleep with Jack like that. You'll crush him."

"I know Mother. You tell me every night!"

Jack squirmed. He didn't like when BT was rude to Mother.

"Well, you may as well get used to it." Mother picked up a sweatshirt from the floor and put it over the desk chair. "Have you finished packing?"

Jack's ears perked up. Was BT really going somewhere? His stomach churned and he wished he had paid more attention to what BT and Mother had talked about in the kitchen earlier.

Memories of the last time BT went away haunted Jack. His leg had got stuck in the heater vent cover. He pulled, pushed, tugged, and even licked his leg to no avail. He was trapped! Jack swore a trickle of sweat got in his eye, even though he was pretty sure guinea pigs don't sweat. When he dropped a few chocolate nuggets on the floor - a true sign of despair - Jack knew the situation was serious.

Try as he might to free his leg, he realized the only way was to chew it off.

All he had to do was open his mouth, put it around the leg and bite down with all his might. He practiced biting quickly and efficiently, hoping somebody would come to the rescue but nobody did. Ok, it was time. Sharp teeth began to dig into his pink flesh and . . . Mother appeared!

What if something horrible happened this time and nobody found him? Out of a morbid curiosity, Jack successfully balanced himself on three legs. He liked to be prepared.

"I already told you. I'm ready," said BT.

"Aieee!" Mother's face scrunched up in pain and she grabbed her foot.

BT and Jack startled. Jack's hind end slipped off BT's shoulder but he caught himself by digging his claws into the fabric of BT's shirt.

"Are you ok?" BT's head turned towards Mother.

"No, I'm not! This wouldn't have happened if you kept your room clean!" Mother tried not to yell. "Benjamin Theodore, I told you to clean up these blocks last night!"

"I didn't mean for you to hurt yourself." BT put Jack down and swiftly tossed the blocks into a plastic bin.

"I'm tired of telling you to clean up this room." Mother pinched her lips together and put her foot on the floor gingerly.

"I'm sorry. I promise I'll try harder." BT picked Jack up and plopped back down onto the beanbag.

"You'd better, or I'll start deducting money from your allowance."

She straightened up the papers and books strewn across BT's desk, then came over and kissed BT on the head. "You know how much I love you, don't you?"

"Yes, mom, I do." BT kept his head still just long enough for the kiss then shrugged it away.

"Have a good night, boys."

She patted Jack's mohawk down before turning towards the door. Jack didn't like hands on the "hawk." He had to lick his paws and sharpen it.

How, exactly, was Jack expected to have a good night? His best friend was leaving. He nestled close to BT's neck - his favorite place to be. There was no need to cry - Jack told himself. Brave guinea pigs never cried.

BT reached up to pet Jack. "I'm glad you're coming with us this time, Jack Attack."

Jack's eyes opened wide and his jaw dropped down to his paws!

CHAPTER 2

Are We There Yet?

The airport was an exciting place, full of humans rushing to and fro. Jack saw other cages, some with dogs and some with cats. He didn't like cats. They smelled bad, really bad. The thought made him gag and he coughed up a bit of hay.

After what seemed a very long time, BT set Jack's cage on the floor and pushed a few celery sticks through the wires. Jack was busy chewing and enjoying the view when a little girl plopped down in front of him. Jack jumped back.

"Look, Mommy, it's a rat!" she said.

Her mother walked over to look at Jack. "It's a guinea pig. You can tell because he doesn't have a long skinny tail."

"Oh, he's pretty. I want one!"

The mother walked away but the girl stayed, stuffing her mouth with something from a box that had a chicken drawn on the side. How insulting! He was nothing like a rat. Every nasty gray rat he saw on television survived by living in sewers and eating garbage, except for the one that was a chef in a fancy restaurant. Jack was intelligent, organized, ate crisp vegetables and had clean orange and white fur.

The young girl chewed with her mouth open. Bits of food fell to the floor. He looked at the chicken on the box and instantly stood a bit taller. He was not food. He was a guinea pig - Beast of the East. Jack was happy to be on his way when BT picked him up again.

They walked through a silver tunnel that opened into a long room filled with seats. BT explained they were on the airplane and that Jack should rest because it would take all day to fly over the Gulf of Mexico, Central America and most of South America until they reached Peru. BT stuffed Jack's cage under his seat. It was so dark. Jack backed himself into a corner and pulled his blanket up over his head.

Jack thought back to last night when BT told him he was going to Peru, too. Jack squealed with delight and relief hit him like a cool breeze. Lucky for him, the television program was still on. He paid close attention to better prepare himself for *Abuela's* house. Jack giggled when he remembered BT rubbing his palms together greedily when he talked about them finding Incan Gold.

Tucked up in the dark corner, Jack busied his mind, making a mental list. The man on the television program said people spoke Spanish in Peru. *Number One: Learn Spanish.* No problem . . . checkmark. Jack had listened while BT studied for his Spanish tests out loud. BT probably didn't know that Jack understood English and Spanish. He was bilingual just like BT and Mother.

Wait just a minute, Jack also spoke Dog! That made him, trilingual. It was all due to that unfortunate near death experience a few months ago, when BT left the front door open and Jack ventured out. He was minding his own business, happily nibbling grass, when he noticed the mangy dog in the neighbor's yard. Jack tensed then cautiously crept back towards the open door.

But, it was too late.

The dog raised his snout and stiffened. His nose was a guinea pig radar detector that instantly spotted Jack. Jack swore he saw the dog smirk before he bounded over BT's scooter and trapped him against the front porch steps. His teeth were as long as Jack's leg bone. Stinky dog saliva dripped onto Jack's forehead and slid down his face. Jack's stomach dropped to the ground completely. How could he protect himself?

"Stop drooling on me!" Jack commanded the dog.

The dog stopped snarling, pulled his head back and looked completely confused.

"Yeah, you heard me. Stop drooling on me!"

The monstrous creature made a warning snap in the direction of Jack, but still had a wary look in his eyes.

"Step back before I saddle you up and ride you like a horse!" Jack stood up on his hind legs and scrunched up his face.

The dog stepped back and cocked his head to one side.

"Scram!" BT yelled when he came out the front door. The dog ran back to his yard, where he sat and watched Jack, who by now was safe in BT's arms. Jack shook the memory back to the depths of his brain.

Jack grinned and reached up to feel his mohawk. If he counted Dog as a language, maybe he should count Guinea Pig, too. He had no idea what word to use for somebody who spoke four languages so he decided to just stick with trilingual.

Jack considered what else should be on his list. *Number Two: Pack Blanket.* He already had it . . . checkmark. *Number Three: Remember What Inca Looks Like.* They would need to be able to recognize an Inca if they were going to find his treasure. He was fairly sure it was safe to checkmark number three. Jack pulled his fuzzy blanket tight and practiced saying his favorite words in Spanish.

Zanahoria – carrot

Apio – celery

Perejil – parsley

. . . until he drifted off to sleep.

There was no protection from the nightmare that dropped Jack into a desperate land. He wandered through a maze of cornstalks and rosemary bushes. The full moon resembled a large paper lantern before it buried itself behind thick clouds, leaving him in near darkness except for a faint light in the distance. Every turn he took hoping to reach it lead him further away.

The light played tricks on him. It was behind him. Then it was in front of him. He ran himself ragged chasing it, but never got close. Eventually, Jack stopped to rest. A chill overcame his body, and from nowhere, a large shadow forced him backwards until rosemary stems prickled his back through his thick fur.

He was trapped!

CHAPTER 3

What on Earth?

The next morning, Jack awoke in a small, bright bedroom. The last thing Jack remembered was BT carrying his cage through the airport and a voice welcoming them to Lima, the capital of Peru.

Two tall windows were cracked open and a cool breeze entered. The air smelled different. Jack lazily stretched his legs and drank from his water bottle. BT was still asleep on the bed.

Knock! Knock! Knock!

A small wrinkled woman stuck her head into the room. Jack jumped and kicked his hind legs out like a bucking bronco. He scrambled under his blanket so only his eyes peeked out. Her dark hair was pulled back from her face and she wore a kind smile. Who was she?

"*Buenos días, hijito,*" she said sweetly.

Jack's eyes moved from her to BT, who stirred awake.

"*Abuela, buenos días,*" said BT.

Abuela, thought Jack. She was Grandmother, *Abuela*.

Abuela kissed BT on the cheek and sat down on the edge of his bed. Jack crept out from under his blanket.

BT's voice sounded strange, and so did *Abuela's*. Words rolled from their mouths differently.

Aha! They were speaking Spanish. Jack was proud of himself because he understood most of what they said. He began to go through his list of words.

Profesor - teacher

Escuela - school

BT was telling *Abuela* about his favorite teacher, Mr. Murray. BT talked about him every day. Jack imagined that Mr. Murray was Superman disguised as a teacher. Mother told her friends that Mr. Murray was good for BT.

BT yanked Jack back to the conversation when he grabbed him from the cage to introduce him to *Abuela*. Jack made sure to open his eyes as wide as possible and was pleased he hadn't yet sharpened his mohawk. *Abuela* picked him up gently and petted him right between the ears with her small hands. Mmph - she smelled good, like *flores* - flowers.

"*Qué lindo cuy,*" said *Abuela*.

Jack squealed softly and batted his eyelashes to let her know he also liked her. Mother always told BT, "You get more flies with sugar." Jack didn't want flies, but he knew what Mother meant.

After *desayuno* - breakfast, BT took Jack outside and set him down in the grass, which he of course nibbled. It was different, sweeter. Jack had never been in such a wondrous place. *Abuela* lived on an *hacienda* - farm. It was surrounded by towering mountains, as far as the eye could see. There were so many different sounds and scents - smoke from a wood-burning fire, fresh dirt with big juicy earth worms, chicken droppings, a nearby vegetable garden and the light wind smelled like the oily balm Mother put on BT's chest when his nose was stuffy. The breeze from another direction carried a strangely familiar scent.

Odd.

What could it be?

Happily there was no hint of cat in the air, although he could deal with one if he had to. He saw how it was done in a movie once. Four super-ninja guinea pigs swung a cat by his tail round and round. When they let go, the cat flew, meowing all the way, into a swimming pool.

Jack flexed and squeezed his biceps. Rock hard, as usual. He decided he may be able to swing a cat all by himself if necessary. He tried to do a push-up, but a blade of grass went up his nose and made him sneeze.

The stone wall that enclosed the yard had different types of pointed sharp cacti growing from the cracks. In the far corner of the yard sat a small stone cottage, the type that was in the fairy tales BT read to him. Hmm, Jack wondered if a good witch or a wicked witch lived inside. Note for list - *Search Stone Cottage*. It was probably where they kept the lawnmower and shovels.

Jack turned towards *Abuela's* house, his jaw dropped. It was huge! It was built of the same stone as the wall, but was as tall as the trees and had big red tiles on the roof. A thrill rushed from his nose to his toes. He licked his front paws and sharpened his orange mohawk. He planned to explore every inch of the property, inside and out. Scratch out last note on list. Add, *Explore Every Inch*. There had to be a thousand secret hiding places waiting to be found.

"*Oye Benjamín, ven aquí un momentito,*" called *Abuela*.

BT went to *Abuela* as asked. She was holding a big box with her small hands. Jack wondered if it was a gift.

BT sat down on the steps and pulled a big cage from

the box. He thanked *Abuela* with a kiss on the cheek.

"Look what *Abuela* bought us, Jack Attack." BT set the cage down on the grass and opened the door. "Wait here. I'm going back inside to get your blanket and toys to put in your new cage."

Jack looked at the cage and sniffed it over before going inside. It was big - maybe too big. He didn't need so much space because he mostly just slept inside. BT let him run around wherever and whenever Jack wanted. Mother didn't like it, but he didn't chew on furniture or leave a trail of his unique chocolate drops on the floor. Ok, except for that one time.

Jack sucked in a squeal and put his paw to his mouth! Maybe *Abuela* would insist he stay in the cage.

No, it couldn't be!

That would most certainly cramp his style.

Jack needed to know if he would be able to come and go as he pleased, so he went inside to try the door. It was heavy, but with effort and extra deep squeals, Jack pulled it closed. He stepped back for a minute to catch his breath then tried to open it. Yikes, the latch was different! He pushed and pulled. He was able to get it half open, then nothing. Jack stomped his front paw in frustration.

Think, Jack Attack, think!

Something to hold it halfway open so he could push it the rest of the way was what Jack needed. He turned around and looked at the empty cage.

Nothing. Nada. Zilch.

He would search for a small stick the next time he was out. The thought of being trapped like a common animal made him shiver and quiver. This new cage was not going to keep him from snooping around and having a good time. Really, what's the use of educating yourself about Peru by watching all that TV if you can't even poke around the backyard?

What's taking BT so long? I want out! Jack scowled and shook the bars with his front paws. He stopped in mid shake, nose in the air, eyes open wide.

There it was again, that oddly familiar scent. It was getting stronger. Jack slowly crept back away from the bars and moved towards the center of the cage. The scent grew stronger and stronger. The ground rumbled. It was getting closer.

What on Earth?

A mighty dust cloud moved through the yard like a herd of horses from the animal programs on television. It curved here and swerved there. Jack stood completely still, eyes glued to the cloud as it screeched to a halt in front of his cage. The head of the jumble stopped dead in his tracks, which caused chaos. They bumped and slid into one another and ended up in a big pile.

Jack stood without blinking, dust burning his eyes. Maybe the cage wasn't so bad, after all.

He felt rather safe inside. Scents overwhelmed his nostrils. They smelled like dirt, sweat, and him!

After the dust cleared, a thin rat-like animal without a tail stalked towards Jack's cage. He was covered in dusty charcoal fur and he twirled his long silver goatee until it hung like an icicle. He circled the cage slowly, in menacing silence, never taking his eyes off Jack.

"What are you?" His voice was a bottomless pit.

Jack was downright frightened. He held back a dust filled cough and wondered how to respond. Swallowing his fear, he looked the other animal in the eye, walked closer to the bars and asked, "What are YOU?"

CHAPTER 4

Delicious and Juicy

They stared at one another until BT opened the door of the house and the herd scattered.

Jack's front paws grabbed the bars. "I love my cage. I love my cage. I love my cage."

"Hey Jack, I see you've met a Wild Pack. I forgot to tell you *Abuela* raises wild guinea pigs. Maybe you'll make some friends!"

Jack was breathless and squeal-less, which was almost impossible. He stared ahead and tried to comprehend BT's words - wild guinea pigs?

That's why their scent was so familiar, although they didn't have muscles like Jack. They were dusty - and where was their cage?

"Hey little buddy, come out for a run." BT said as he opened the cage door.

Fear was exhausting, but Jack had just enough energy to search the grass for a twig while BT prepared the new cage. As soon as it was ready, Jack walked inside and snuggled in for a nap. He patted his blanket to make sure the twig was there. It was the key to his freedom -- that is, if he dared go out.

Curiosity kept Jack from napping even though his cage was back inside their bedroom. For as long as he could remember, Jack had only lived with humans. What would it be like to hang out with the Wild Pack? They surely wouldn't attack him. They were guinea pigs – Jack was a guinea pig. He could walk up, offer his paw and introduce himself. They would welcome him.

Why wouldn't they? He was intelligent and liked to have fun, plus his mohawk was super cool like the ninja-guinea pigs in the movies.

Jack dreamed they would make him their king or give him an Incan treasure - maybe a golden staff or jeweled crown. They may even give him a necklace made of solid gold peanuts like he saw on television. Jack's smile turned to a frown. There was a problem with his dream - and that *problem* had a goatee and a seriously bad attitude.

Jack's sense of adventure conquered his fear of the scary grey guinea. What was the worst that could happen? Jack could always turn around and run back to *Abuela's*, right?

It was time to pull out the twig. He opened the latch as far as he could and jammed in the twig to help him wedge it open all the way.

Success!

Jack did his signature dance. He looked over his right shoulder and shook his round furry rump, while he sang.

"Beast, beast of the East!
Go Ja-ack!
Go Ja-ack!
Go, go, go Ja-ack!"

He ended with three little hops, and sauntered out.

Jack crawled, pulled and grunted himself up to the windowsill to get an aerial view of the yard. On the other side of the stone wall next to the cottage, a herd of alpaca was corralled in a pen.

He squished his face against the window for a better view. A man, wearing a large brimmed hat, was holding an alpaca still while another man shaved it. When the man finished, he tossed the big bunch of fur onto a pile. The shorn alpaca jumped up and ran. The animal looked quite strange with a shaved body and furry head.

So, this must be where Mother gets her boxes of alpaca fur. *Abuela* probably sends them to Knoxville. Jack knew *Abuela* sent crates of asparagus to the organic grocery store where Mother shopped, back home. Whenever Mother

bought it, she called it *espárragos de la abuela* - grandma's asparagus.

It made Jack happy to see the animals set free after the sheering. Mother told people no animals were killed to make the clothing sold in her store, but it was good for Jack to see for himself. A guinea pig can't believe everything he hears.

The Wild Pack was nowhere to be found. Where were those grey guinea pigs? Who closed this window? If he could only get the window open he may be able to pick up their scent. Ha! That wasn't going to happen. Even though he was the Guinea Beast of the East, his arms just weren't long enough.

Jack remembered smelling vegetables when he was outside. Surely, if he found the garden, he would find the Wild Pack. No guinea pig could resist fresh veggies. Tips of corn stalks stood high enough for Jack to see. They were beyond the wall on the backside of the house. If the Wild Pack wasn't there, at least he would have a snack. His muscular belly rumbled.

It was surprisingly easy to sneak out of *Abuela's* house. Most of the doors and windows on the first floor were open. The sound of music filled the home. It was completely different than the music BT listened to with his friends - and not just because the words were in Spanish. When he crept past the *comedor* – dining room, where the humans were eating, he heard *Abuela* talking about the eucalyptus trees that grew all over the Andes Mountains.

When Jack heard the words "Andes Mountains," *montañas*, he was reminded that the Inca lived there. If he saw an Inca out in the yard, he would follow him to his treasure and put off his search for the Wild Pack until tomorrow. He snickered to himself and thought he would probably have a thing or two to teach the Wild

Pack about Peru, unless they had also watched the weeklong special on their television.

BT told Jack that *Abuela* served *almuerzo* – lunch, at 3:00 in the afternoon, and that it was their largest meal of the day. *Cena* – dinner was served at 8:00 at night and was more like a typical lunch back in Knoxville. *Abuela* was serving *Trucha Frita* - fried trout for *almuerzo* today and Jack would most certainly taste it for his bedtime snack tonight. Jack licked his lips. The dining room smelled delicious! He would be back in plenty of time. It was still daylight and he never stayed out after dark.

Almuerzo
3:00
Trucha Frita
Papas
Ensalada

Jack stepped down onto the small porch just outside the door leading to the yard. He cautiously looked around - prepared to react in

44

case of danger. He didn't sense the Wild Pack but there was a strange noise coming from the back corner of the yard. He ran as fast as his muscular legs would carry him to the stone cottage. He was out of breath by the time he got there but thought it was the safest way to cross the open space.

Jack stepped inside and sniffed the air. He didn't see the Wild Pack, but there was a strong odor coming from a patch of straw. It smelled like sweaty, dirty guinea pig and, oh, nasty, guinea pee! Disgusting! Jack had a specific pee spot in one corner of his cage. He was too civilized to go just anywhere!

Jack roamed the little cottage to see what was making the loud noise. He crawled onto a pile of wooden crates in one corner and saw a woman standing at a big stone wheel that was spinning very fast. She picked up a large butcher knife and put the edge of the blade to the stone. Sparks flew in all directions and the screech made

Jack cover his ears. She picked up one knife after another until she finished them all and turned off the wheel. Then she put a whole watermelon on the table and picked up the largest knife. She raised her arm way above her head and came down, cutting the melon in half with one chop. She smelled so strongly of onions that Jack could barely smell the sweet watermelon.

"Squeak!"

The woman turned towards Jack. She still had the knife in hand.

Jack heard her call out "guinea pig" in Spanish. She was a short woman with the largest hands and feet he had ever seen and she was coming his way! Jack jumped from the crates and dashed away.

"¡Cuy rico y jugoso! ¡Ven aquí!"

Why was she calling him delicious and juicy?

Jack froze when he heard the words. That's what he called a big piece of celery, a radish or yummy booger snack.

He wasn't food!

He wasn't a chicken!

The sound of her footsteps snapped him back to life and he ran out the door and dove into a pile of wood. Jack held his breath until the woman turned and went back into the cottage.

Everything in Peru was unfamiliar to Jack. BT told him the visit would be full of adventure, but he didn't say anything about danger lurking around every corner. A wave of panic threatened him. *Number Five: Never Go In Cottage*

He took a deep breath and poked his head out to have a look. There was no scent of onion in the air. The gate leading to the vegetables was nearby, but *Abuela's* house was just across the yard. Jack looked from one to the other. He knew what to expect if he went back to the house. He would wait around for BT to finish lunch. Then they would maybe spend time together, which Jack really enjoyed, BUT, he was closer to the gate.

CHAPTER 5

Hunt For the Wild Pack

It was a tight squeeze, but Jack made it under the wooden gate. He looked to the right and saw vegetables. He looked to the left and saw vegetables. He didn't know where to begin so he pranced around a very tall artichoke plant laughing and squealing.

He was so excited that he leapt twelve inches off the ground. He squeaked when he landed and thought that must be a world record leap.

There were potatoes, green and red cabbages, beets, tall stalks of juicy corn, asparagus, tomatoes, celery which he stopped to nibble, broccoli, peppers, lettuce, strawberries and spinach among many other incredible plants. It was like being in a huge tossed salad!

Jack ate and ate and ate until his belly was sick. He needed to rest and the stack of hay bales on the edge of the garden seemed the perfect spot if only he could get his fat belly to the top. As he climbed, it dragged and swayed.

Overeating was a mistake Jack knew all too well. Last year, he found peanut butter cookies forgotten on the bedroom floor. He had no business finishing off the entire box.

But he did.

That was a bad day, and thinking about it made his stomach even worse. He made it to the top of the stack and lay down to rest.

• ● •

Jack startled awake. A shiver ran up his spine knowing the huge-handed woman could have easily captured him. He stood up and stretched his legs, relieved that his belly no longer dragged on the hay, though he was still very full.

Jack looked toward the sky and saw the sun was low and the shadows were long. He had to find the Wild Pack soon because he wanted to be back in the house with BT before dark. Even though Jack craved adventure, he wasn't crazy.

Who knew what animals roamed *Abuela's* farm at night? Jack would have a sad ending if he met up with a real jaguar! Some of the information he remembered from television was coming in handy on this adventure. *Number Six: Avoid Jaguars*.

Jack stood up on his hind paws. A wide dirt path ran from the wooden gate through the garden and out of sight. Maybe if Jack followed it, he would find the Wild Pack.

He was careful to stay along the edge of the path to be ready to jump into the vegetables if there was any sign of trouble. Really he had no interest in food at the moment. The thought was nauseating.

The path quickly became narrow and headed downhill. Each side was lined by a stone wall. He walked out onto one and saw that *Abuela's* farm was nothing like the flat farms he was familiar with. Her crops grew on huge steps carved into the mountain on each side of the narrow path. Each step was covered with different plants. The one below him was oats and the one below that was sweet potato. This step-gardening continued on down the mountain as far as Jack could see. It was marvelous! He had never seen anything like it, not even on television. The blocks of different shades of green and gold looked like the quilt on Mother's bed.

In the distance, there were tree-covered mountains and above them, higher mountains with snow-topped peaks. A deep breath of fresh air invigorated Jack, but eucalyptus wasn't the only scent on the breeze. The Wild Pack was near. He jumped down to the next large step and hid among the oats.

The Wild Pack made quite a racket scurrying up the narrow path between the large steps. Jack wasn't sure what to do. Should he jump out and surprise them? Maybe that was not such a good idea. Should he follow them from a distance? No, what was the point of that? They would think he was afraid.

Jack ran up to the garden to wait for them on the path. He was out of breath by the time he arrived. All this running and unlimited tasty veggies were going to kill him. When he heard them approach, he posed himself against an artichoke plant. He knew he looked cool like this because he practiced in front of the mirror in his bedroom back in Knoxville and tough humans posed like this all the time on TV.

The Wild Pack came charging up the path. The guinea pig in the lead screeched to a halt and the others landed in a pile. Jack shook his head and rolled his eyes.

"You think you're a hot shot, don't you?" The guinea pig who was leading the Wild Pack stared Jack in the eye. He was the same scary one from *Abuela's* yard.

"As a matter of fact, I do," said Jack. He was using his deepest voice.

"What are you?" asked the guinea pig.

"You ask the wrong question. Not *what* am I, but *who* am I?" Jack stood up and put his paws on his hips. "They call me Jack . . . I'm the Roughest, Toughest, Orange, Mohawkiest Guinea Beast of the East!"

The Wild Pack let out a frightened squeal in unison and cowered back.

"Well, Jack, my name is Pablo, and I am the leader of this pack and this area." He stepped towards Jack, stood up on his hind paws and puffed his chest out. "Where is your pack, Jack?" Pablo's eyes gleamed with threat.

Jack thought, really, where is my pack? Why don't I have a pack?   He didn't want to show his confusion so he let out a low growl and smirked. "I don't need a pack." Then . . . .

SWOOP!

SWISH!

SWOOP!

"Run!" yelled Pablo.
Jack looked over his shoulder and saw a huge hand at the other end of a net. "Not her again!"

Jack ran for his life with the Wild Pack, or tried to. They were so quick. Jack bumped around like a pinball between them until he was finally pushed out the back.

It was almost dark by the time the pack stopped running. Whew! Jack was huffing and puffing and none of them were. He was out of shape compared to the Wild Pack. If he was going to run with them he needed to be a bit less muscular.

Pablo stood beside a small hut made from rough bricks. He motioned for the other guinea pigs to step inside. "You may as well come in, too, Jack, unless, of course, you don't need a pack," said Pablo.

Jack walked past Pablo. He made sure to maintain his composure but turned off the sassy attitude. He was grateful, after all, that the Wild

Pack led him to safety, but how would he get back to BT? He was probably looking for him all over the house.

It was so dark outside. Jack swallowed a lump of fear.

CHAPTER 6

Guinea Pigs Are Not Food

The doorway led to a cozy room with a straw-covered floor. There must have been twenty guinea pigs, all seated in a circle, but Jack chose to lean against the wall near the door. The guineas were focused on Pablo when he marched through the room. Pablo didn't look anybody in the eye until he reached the far corner and turned towards his pack. Jack was sure to pay close attention, just like he did when watching TV with BT.

"That was too close!" The seriousness of the situation was evident in Pablo's voice. "The pack is no longer permitted to go near the yard during daylight hours."

A small grey guinea pig cautiously raised her paw.

"Yes, ask your question." Pablo softened his tone.

"*Cocinera* has never tried to capture us at dusk. Why would she do that?"

"I've been thinking. I heard her call out 'Juicy Jack!'" He then pointed directly at Jack. "*Cocinera* wants *him*!"

The pack inhaled sharply and turned to look at Jack.

"What? Why would she want me?" Jack was concerned about Pablo's comment but didn't want to appear afraid. "Well, I can understand why she would want me over you all." Jack shook his mohawk and leaned back against the wall.

"Yes. Yes. Now I understand why *Cocinera* wants you," said Pablo. "You are so fat! She wants to suck the marrow from your bones!"

Shocked squeals erupted.

Pablo stared at Jack, but Jack didn't show how intimidated he really was.

Pablo pointed his paw to the door. "Everybody will graze on the lower terraces tonight, but make

sure to stay away from the asparagus. It's tall now, and the humans could show up at any time to harvest." The Wild Pack immediately did as commanded.

Jack didn't change the expression on his face, nor did he meet the eyes of the pack that passed by. To tell the truth, Jack wasn't feeling the least bit confident of his situation. He reached up - his mohawk was even a bit flat. He went out, as well, but didn't follow the pack down the steep path. He went to the side of the hut and sat against the wall. He didn't understand life on *Abuela's* farm. He should never have left his cage and come in search of the Wild Pack.

Jack needed a plan. He knew he should start by examining his list. *Number Four: explore every inch of the farm*, had to be scratched off. What should he put on *Number Seven*? The list seemed foolish. It belonged in another world, the safe tidy one back in Knoxville.

At this very moment, BT was probably worried about him. If Jack went up the path towards *Abuela's* house, maybe he would find BT outside looking for him. Although, if BT wasn't in the yard and *Cocinera* was . . . . Jack couldn't finish the thought. It was too frightening. Pablo did tell his pack not to go close to the yard during the day. Maybe it was safe, now that it was dark. An owl screeched overhead - Jack cowered. He didn't want to ask Pablo for help. He wouldn't!

A grey guinea pig walked up the path. Jack quickly sat up straight because she was coming his way. She handed him a bunch of barley. It smelled yummy. Jack thanked her in a voice that expressed no emotion. He noticed her fur was clean. All of the guinea pigs from the Wild Pack had been clean.

Though Jack didn't invite her to sit next to him, she did.

"I'm Eva."

Jack finished a mouthful of barley before speaking. "It's nice to meet you, Eva. I'm Jack."

"I know your name. What I want to know is why you're here?"

Jack didn't like Eva's tone of voice but he would try to be polite because he needed information, and she was very cute. She had short grey fur with an unusual white crescent moon on the middle of her forehead. He turned to look her in the eye. "Let me repeat myself. It's nice to meet you, Eva."

She didn't seem to know how to respond and let a low grunt slip out before regaining her composure. "It's nice to meet you too, Jack."

Strange, she sounded intelligent. "To answer your question, I am here on vacation. My *Abuela* lives in the big house up there." He pointed to where he thought the house may be.

"Your *abuela*?"

"Well she's BT's *Abuela*."

"Who's BT?"

"His full name is Booger Toe and he's my best friend. He's my human. We share a bedroom. His bed is much larger, of course. Mine is inside my cage." Jack wished he were in his cage right now, snuggling his fuzzy blanket.

"A ca-age!" Her entire body tensed and her face twisted with horror.

"Yes, a cage. It's all very civilized. We live in the city, not on the side of some mountain." Jack spat out the words and lifted his right paw up to emphasize their surroundings.

"So you are implying that guinea pigs that live in the mountains are not civilized?" Eva stood back from Jack. She had an offended look on her face and one paw on her hip.

This conversation was going downhill and fast. Jack didn't want to admit that he needed the Wild Pack, but in the back of his mind, he knew the truth. Come on Jack, think before you speak.

He would change his approach with these wild guinea pigs. Maybe they were only "wild" in the sense that they lived outdoors, in the wild. Jack thought more as he chewed his barley. Really, they didn't live in the wild. They were *Abuela's* guinea pigs and they obviously had a hut, which was just a glorified cage in his opinion, though, he would not say that to Eva. She would most certainly get mad. Even though the hut didn't have a television, Jack did appreciate that it didn't have a door to be opened and closed.

Jack slightly bowed his head to Eva. "Now it's my turn to apologize for being rude."

"Apology accepted," she replied.

"First and foremost, does *Cocinera* really want to . . . eat . . . me?" Jack knew that *cocinera* did mean cook.

"She's the *cocinera* at *Abuela's* house, as you call it. We belong to *Abuela*, along with the goats, chickens and alpaca that live on the upper terraces, the ones without vegetables. We stick to the lower terraces - the corn, wheat and vegetable fields on the side of the mountain."

Jack's mind almost exploded when Eva said chickens.

"Please correct me if I'm wrong. You put your guinea pack in the same category as the chickens? Does *Abuela* eat them? Does she eat guinea pigs?" His mohawk fell flat and his eyes pleaded with her to answer no.

But she didn't.

"Of course, *Abuela* eats goats, chickens and guinea pigs! Sometimes she even eats an alpaca, but mostly they are raised for their fur. We haven't lost one from our pack for the last two years. Pablo keeps us safe and our hut is a bit far from *Abuela's* house. *Cocinera* is lazy, lazy, lazy."

Jack stared at Eva in disbelief.

"A pack was moved up to the stone cottage in the yard, but we haven't seen them for awhile. Pablo suspects the worst," continued Eva.

Would BT eat guinea pig? Jack's stomach lurched. He really didn't want to vomit in front of Eva. That would *not* be cool!

Oh, no, it was coming! Jack put his paw to his mouth, hoping to hold it in.

"Eva!" Pablo approached with anger written all over his face.

This can't be happening was Jack's last thought before - Baaarrff!! All of those vegetables Jack shoveled in were now sitting on Pablo's front paws.

"You absolutely disgust me, Juicy Jack!" said Pablo.

Eva's mouth and eyes were wide open. Jack was humiliated! He had never been so un-cool in his entire life.

"Eva, to the hut!" Pablo spoke through snarling teeth.

Eva startled and jumped at least twenty inches in the air.

"Yes father." Eva didn't look Pablo in the eye and if she'd had a tail, it would've been between her legs as she tiptoed away.

Oh no, Pablo is Eva's Father!

Wow, can she jump!

Not only did Jack vomit in front of Eva, but she left his world record jump of 12 inches in the dust. Could Jack's day get any worse? Pablo stared at Jack until Eva crawled into the hut. Just before she rounded the corner, she peeked back. Jack noted a look of sympathy in her eyes.

Pablo was not happy.

CHAPTER 7

Who Needs a Pack?

"If you know what's good for you, you'll stay right here, Juicy Jack!" Pablo turned and ran off into the dark, up and away from the terraces.

Jack wasn't accustomed to being outside at night without his family. He squirmed but couldn't get comfortable on the cold hard dirt. He missed BT terribly. Jack's mind went back to Pablo's nasty words, asking him where his pack was.

"I do have a pack!" BT and Mother were his pack, and boy, oh boy, did he need them - right now, in fact.

There was no chance the Wild Pack was going to give him a solid gold peanut. It probably didn't have one. Maybe gold peanuts didn't even exist. BT always reminded Jack that not everything on television was true. The Wild Pack could have welcomed him, but it didn't. That was the most disappointing. He secretly hoped to make at least one guinea pig friend, but in reality, Jack was sitting alone and felt very unsure of life on *Abuela's* farm. Sure, he knew many things, but not what he needed to know to safely do as he pleased in Peru.

Maybe he wasn't as savvy as he believed. Jack spoke many languages and knew about treasures, the Inca, and many other interesting facts, but he hadn't had the opportunity to share them with the Wild Pack.

As for how tough he thought he was, he wasn't, though he would never say that out loud. The Wild Pack ran faster, jumped higher and kept away from *Cocinera*. Jack had almost been captured and eaten twice. How did Eva jump so high? She was small and thin, that had to be it. Maybe if he ate a bit less and got more exercise, he would become less muscular.

Jack couldn't sit still any longer, so he went behind the hut to practice. His first jump was only about 10 inches high. He concentrated, did a few squats then continued to practice. Each time he landed, his muscles jiggled like jelly. After Jack reached a new record jump of 13 inches and was in the middle of his signature dance, a guinea pig walked by. The guinea looked at Jack like he was crazy and scurried off. It seemed to Jack as though he couldn't do anything right.

No matter, he continued. The next jump was even higher, at 14 inches. Jack smiled. He planned to eat a bit less until his belly stopped swaying, and vowed to practice at least ten jumps each day. Surely this would improve his skills. Obviously, from watching Eva, guinea pigs were good jumpers and he most definitely wanted to jump higher than she.

"One last jump," said Jack.

It wasn't a particularly high jump, but he landed with his back leg twisted in a hole. He grabbed his paw and rubbed it. Voices were coming from the hole. He squeezed in until he clearly heard Eva speaking with another guinea pig. It wasn't considered eavesdropping because Jack heard his name.

"You know your father is a very watchful guinea pig," said an unknown voice.

Eva let out a low grunting squeal. "I know, Mom, you tell me all the time."

"It's for your own protection, so you may as well get used to it. The pack's safety is a daily concern on this farm."

"When will he return?" asked Eva.

"As soon as he's ready to deal with this Jack situation."

"Of course. I'm going down to the lower terraces. Father's not here to stop me and I'm hungry."

Jack pushed himself from the tunnel and secretly followed Eva. She scurried down the dirt path, taking two steps at a time. Jack was amazed and couldn't keep his eyes off her. Eva was full of energy and her fur was shiny under the moonlight.

Jack had never seen stars shine so bright.

Eva stopped at the barley field next to another guinea pig. "Hey, save some for me."

"I've been waiting for you. What's going on up there?" asked the other guinea.

Eva waited to speak until she swallowed her food. "Just Pablo trying to control my life - the usual."

"What about that fat guinea - Jack?"

"What about him?" said Eva.

"He's very handsome."

"I guess, if you like pumpkin-colored fur."

"I do like it. It's more interesting than our boring grey fur," said the other guinea.

"Well, he's likely to disappear soon, so don't get too used to him. If he isn't served for dinner he'll just be going back from wherever he came," said Eva.

"I've never heard a guinea speak like him. His accent is almost like the goats *Abuela* brought from the United States last year. Maybe that's where he's from."

"Why don't you ask him, if you're so curious?"

"I think I will." The other guinea smiled at Eva.

"Ha! Pablo will get on your case, too, if you do." Eva smirked. "Remember how mad he was at me earlier in the year?"

"Well, I won't make that mistake. You should have known better than to hang out with that jungle guinea," said the other guinea. "Do you think Pablo knows how you dream of leaving our pack for an adventure? Maybe I'll tell him."

Eva growled and walked to another plant. A loud squeal sounded from the hut. Jack immediately turned his head and dove into the wheat terrace.

Eva had a serious look on her face when she passed. What was going on? He scrambled uphill. Maybe Pablo realized that Jack was gone. That would be bad, really bad.

Guinea voices grew louder as Jack neared the hut. He didn't want to be seen so he scurried through a corn terrace and shinned up a corn stalk very slowly. It was hard for a guinea to shinny. The stone wall was a struggle, but Jack made it over and rushed behind the hut in the nick of time.

"Where were you, Juicy Jack?" Pablo accused.

"I've been right here, behind the hut, exercising." Jack did a push-up. "My name is Jack, not Juicy Jack."

"I will call you Juicy Jack as long as you're a threat to my pack!" Pablo roared. "Stop exercising. You'll need what little energy you have in that fat juicy body of yours. I would hate to see *Cocinera* use your leg bone as a toothpick. From what I hear, she has quite a collection."

CHAPTER 8

A Pack Is a Pack Is a Pack

Eva and a few other guineas came around the corner, but stayed back to listen. Pablo saw them and began to speak. "I went to the top of the garden. *Cocinera* was still there."

The guineas grunted and whispered to one another. Pablo held up his paws to quiet them and told them not to worry. *Cocinera* hadn't seen him. "I've never seen her in the garden, at night. She must know that Juicy Jack is not inside *Abuela's* house because his ca-age is empty." The guineas shrank back and sucked in their breath when Pablo stressed the word cage.

"On a positive note, *Cocinera* doesn't know that Juicy Jack is with our pack, or she would've walked down here for him, as well as for us. We must take action to make sure that Juicy Jack gets back to his cage safely." Pablo stared into Jack's eyes. "I will have no guinea blood on my hands, not even a guinea that I dislike."

Jack sighed with relief but quickly looked at the other guineas hoping they didn't notice. So, the Wild Pack was going to help him! He had been very wrong about not needing a pack.

Pablo called a group of guineas together and they disappeared into the darkness. Jack wasn't included. He would have to be patient.

As soon as Pablo was out of site, the guinea pig that spoke to Eva down on the barley terrace walked towards Jack. Just as she was about to speak, Eva called out, "Mom, is asking for you in the hut." The guinea turned and stomped away.

Eva stayed.

"I guess you know Pablo is my father." Eva gave her head a sassy shake as if she expected trouble.

"Yes, you could've warned me," said Jack.

"He has many other guinea children, but I'm his eldest daughter and his favorite. He's very protective of us all, as you can see."

"Eva, I've been thinking about your pack, and, my family is my pack. We're not so different, even though I'm the only guinea pig in my family. Pablo is protective, but that's what a father does. From what I see, he's good at it," said Jack. "We don't have a father. Mother protects us."

Eva's face showed surprise at Jack's words. Jack was surprised as well. Where did that come from?

It was true. A father protects the family at all costs. Jack learned that from a movie, not from life. Sometimes he heard BT talk about his father. He died when BT was young, just before Jack joined the family.

"You surprise me, Juicy Jack. I mean, Jack," said Eva.

"And you surprise me, Eva." Jack licked one paw and swiped his bang straight upward out of his eye.

"Hey, what's in your fur?" Eva squinted to get a better look at the fur between Jack's ears.

"What do you mean?"

"I didn't notice before, but you have a white lightning bolt on your fur," said Eva.

"No, I don't," said Jack.

"Here, let me see." Eva put her paws on Jack's fur and made it into a shark fin-shaped mohawk. "Since you always make a mohawk like this, your handsome lightning bolt can't be seen." She then swiped her paw up the front. "Now, I can see the bolt!"

"Really?" Jack perked up and smiled. Too bad he didn't have a mirror.

"If I had longer fur, the crescent moon on my forehead probably wouldn't be so clear," said Eva.

This was his first friendly conversation with another guinea pig. He wondered if Eva was enjoying the conversation as much as he was.

"So, Jack, where are you..."

Pablo returned and the happy moment immediately ended. Pablo looked from Jack to Eva. The smile disappeared from Eva's face and she looked down to her front paws. The look on Pablo's face and Eva's reaction nearly made Jack feel guilty for having enjoyed himself.

"I want you away from my pack as soon as possible, Juicy Jack," said Pablo.

Jack noticed that Pablo looked up at the lightning bolt then looked back to his eyes with more menace, if that were even possible.

"I have a plan to return you to your cage - a dangerous plan," said Pablo.

CHAPTER 9

Ready for Fun

A sleek grey guinea dug with his front paws at the edge of the stone wall. Dirt flew everywhere. The guinea pulled out a burlap bundle full of ropes and small daggers. He handed them to three other guineas and Pablo. They expertly tied their weapons to their bodies while Pablo went over the plan one more time. They looked like cowboys Jack had seen on TV - without hats and horses, of course.

The plan was to sneak up the edge of the path and through the yard to get Jack back to *Abuela's* house under the cover of darkness. It would be too easy for *Cocinera* to catch them during the day.

Pablo instructed the Wild Pack that nobody was to go to sleep inside the hut, because that would be the first place *Cocinera* would look for them. They should keep alert for any trouble.

"If the plan fails, scatter. We'll meet in the usual spot, down on the lower terraces." Pablo looked each member of his pack in the eye as he spoke.

"No weapons for you, Juicy Jack. Your belly is so big it drags on the ground, and besides, you're too slow already."

Pablo, Jack and the three other guineas started up the narrow path and out of site of the hut. It was a steep climb, but Jack put forth his best effort to keep up. It wasn't easy. *Number Seven: Survive*. There would be no more points on the list. Jack's survival was the only thing that mattered.

"Hide!" commanded Pablo.

Everybody jumped into the strawberry patch. Jack hadn't noticed the owl overhead but felt the cool gust of wind from the flapping wings.

"Don't move a muscle!" Pablo unsheathed his dagger - ready to fight.

Jack was afraid. He had to remind himself to breathe. His heart was pounding like a hammer. The owl swooped again and flew away with an unfortunate animal wiggling in his talons. Thankfully, it was too big to be a guinea pig. Nonetheless, he shook to rid himself of the chill running up his spine.

"Alright, move out." Pablo quietly ordered. He kept his dagger at the ready.

They were once again on their way up the path. Jack was relieved he wasn't the leader. Even he had to admit that Pablo's senses were exceptional, exactly what they needed to deliver him to *Abuela's* house safely.

Pablo was in front. Jack followed and the three others watched his back. They marched on stopping once more when a rabbit crossed their path.

"The night is alive with hungry creatures of all sizes," said Pablo.

Even though Jack was tense with fear, he realized he was on the adventure of a lifetime. Nothing like this ever happened back in Knoxville. Jack's thoughts suddenly went to BT. Maybe he'd met an Inca or found treasure. Hopefully Jack would make it safely back to *Abuela's* so BT could tell him about his day and Jack could snuggle up close and listen. Jack licked his lips and thought about the

crusty bedtime snack he'd missed tonight. Surely
it would have been delicious.

The path leveled off. They must be nearing the gate. Get your mind back in the game, Jack said to himself.

"Take cover!" commanded Pablo.

Pablo and Jack hid among carrot tops, and the others concealed themselves under a berry bush. Pablo held up his finger for silence. *Cocinera* walked through the gate into the yard.

"That was close." Pablo whispered quietly, as though he were telling only himself. He gave the signal to the other guineas to remain under cover until further notice.

Jack pretended not to hear when Pablo let a quiet squeal of relief slip out. So, Pablo is only a guinea pig, after all. He's not a super-guinea.

As soon as that thought popped into Jack's head, he felt ashamed. Pablo and the other guineas were risking their lives for him. Why? Jack had been nothing but an ill-mannered problem for Pablo and the Wild Pack.

"Juicy Jack . . . you ready for some fun?" Pablo twisted his goatee.

Fun? The temperature seemed to drop. Did anything make Pablo nervous?

Anxiety overpowered Jack's brain. He was on the verge of peeing all over his furry self. Pablo had already proven himself as a leader. Trust was vital, for now, at least. Jack was part of this mission too, even if he was weaker than the others.

Jack took a deep breath and told himself, "You are the Roughest, Toughest, Orange, Mohawkiest Guinea Beast of the East." Then he licked his front paws and sharpened his mohawk like never before. He remembered the lightning bolt and did a quick swipe just up the front.

"Now, I'm ready for some fun!" Jack said with confidence.

Pablo motioned for one of the other guineas to follow him. "Juicy Jack, stay here until I call for you. We'll secure the area."

Pablo and his lieutenant carefully approached the corner of the gate where they stopped to listen. Then they crawled under and out of sight. A few seconds passed, followed by a thump and muffled guinea grunts. The two other grey guineas looked at one another then scurried to the corner of the gate. Slowly they crawled under. Again, a few seconds passed, followed by a second thump and more muffled guinea grunts.

"Te chapé, cuy rico y jugoso!" said *Cocinera*.

Jack saw the top half of the cook's body on the other side of the gate. She jumped up and down with her sacked victims in one hand and a lantern in the other. Then she disappeared into the darkness.

Numbness crept through Jack's body and he felt so heavy he might sink to the ground and never be able to pull himself up again. His mind was almost as blank as the night was dark. Thoughts of being alone and vulnerable popped

into his head as quickly as he tried to push them away. Slowly, he lifted each paw, one by one, trying to bring focus back into his world. He had to move.

Jack knew *Abuela's* house was beyond the gate where BT was surely asleep. *Cocinera* probably took the guineas to the cottage. Maybe this was a good time to dart across the yard to the safety of BT. *Cocinera* had called out "Juicy Jack." She probably thought Jack was in her sack.

He took two steps towards the gate and stopped. He coughed and choked. A tear rolled down his cheek. Then the dam broke and Jack cried. His neck slowly turned down the path towards the hut where the rest of the Wild Pack waited for news of the mission. Who said "Brave guinea pigs don't cry," anyway? Jack knew what he had to do. Scratch *Number Seven*.

CHAPTER 10

Be Careful What You Wish For

Jack blazed down the path, sometimes taking two steps at a time. He must have been making quite a racket because Eva and a crowd of guineas met him outside the hut with concerned looks on their faces.

"Caught . . . All . . . Help!"

"What?" Eva's eyes filled with horror.

"*Cocinera* has them!"

"We have to save them!" called out another guinea.

Eva turned and four other guineas stepped up to volunteer for the rescue mission. Another tossed them ropes and handed them daggers. This time, Jack was given a dagger. It made him feel like a ninja. He hoped he would know how to use it, if necessary.

The Pack took off up the path, not taking time to strap them on. Jack clenched his dagger between his teeth and so did Eva. They looked ferocious!

Jack was determined to save Pablo and the other guineas. He hoped Eva would have a good plan by the time they got to the garden gate.

Jack, Eva and the other guineas stopped under the rosemary bushes at the top of the garden. They stood still and looked to Jack. They were looking to him as he had seen them look to Pablo. Did they expect Jack to lead the rescue mission?

That was not a good idea!

The desperate looks on the guineas' faces reminded Jack that this was what he had wanted - to be their king, their leader. Now Jack wasn't so sure. Mother always warned BT to be careful what he wished for.

Nobody had ever depended on Jack. Quite the opposite was true. He depended on BT and Mother for everything. Jack was afraid at what lay beyond the garden gate, but exhilarated that he was needed. He didn't want to let the Wild Pack down. He reminded himself he was an intelligent guinea pig. In order to form a well thought out plan, Jack would need to consider everything he had learned about the farm and *Cocinera* so far.

Jack composed his thoughts. There was no way they were going under the gate like the others had. They needed to know if *Cocinera* and her net were waiting on the other side. He directed two guineas to climb the stone wall as lookouts. Jack and Eva waited for the signal that the coast was clear.

When Jack and Eva crawled under the gate, they saw hay bales positioned as a trap and four daggers on the ground, one bent beyond repair. They decided to climb over the bales and jump down the other side, just in case.

It was the darkest time of night, just before the sun woke. Jack was a bit rattled but stood still for his heart to calm down enough to listen. Noise was coming from the other side of the yard and light was coming from the cottage. Jack and Eva looked at each other and carefully crept in that direction, keeping to the edge of the stone wall for protection. Jack motioned to one of the lookouts who quickly jumped down to join their search-and-rescue party.

The guineas stealthily approached the stone cottage. Jack peeked through a mouse hole. *Cocinera* was too busy chopping onions to notice him. Pablo and the guineas were nowhere in sight. Jack tried to rely on his sense of smell to locate them, but the scent of onions and smoke from the cooking fire was thick.

Jack slithered inside. Eva and the grey guinea followed. Eva slowly scanned the room. Her eyes stopped on a large cook pot high atop an old wooden crate. Jack followed her gaze and saw the lid pop up then close again. They watched and it popped back up. They saw a small paw and the end of a rope before it closed again. Jack thought for a minute about the situation. He smiled and pulled his friends into a huddle.

Luck was on their side because *Cocinera* had her back to them. Jack and the grey guinea climbed to the top of a woodpile while Eva scampered to a corner of the crate, out of *Cocinera's* sight. Jack gave the grey guinea a look that said, "Here goes nothing," and jumped onto the crate. The grey guinea followed without making a sound. They

quickly scurried to the aluminum pot that held
their friends captive.

How could they let Pablo know they were
there without making too much noise? The grey

guinea scratched at the pot hoping their friends would understand. It was important to be quiet so as not to alert *Cocinera*, or they would all be breakfast.

Jack and the grey guinea listened and heard a scratching sound coming from inside. Great! The captives understood. It was time to get on with the rescue. Jack and the grey guinea began to push the pot to the edge of the crate. It was very heavy. They pushed and shoved and shoved and pushed until it teetered on the edge. Just one last push, and over it went.

The pot landed with a bang and bounced around. The lid flew off and spun like a top, *Cocinera* turned. Pablo and the guineas rolled from the pot. Eva grabbed her father and the others and shoved them towards the mouse hole.

"Jugoso!" *Cocinera* roared and stepped towards Jack with a sharp knife dripping with onion juice.

The watermelon came to Jack's mind and he knew he had to move fast. Jack jumped from the crate, stumbled and rolled. He looked towards the mouse hole and saw the Wild Pack wasn't completely passed through yet. He had to draw attention away from them and find another way out for himself.

Jack headed straight for the door. It was open just a crack. He had never, ever run so fast in his life. He rounded the corner of the shack and was headed for the gate when the cool swoosh of *Cocinera's* net made the fur on his back stick up even more. For a split second Jack looked back and saw *Cocinera* trip over one of her own traps. She was screaming with rage.

Run Run Run!

Cocinera landed in a clump but got back on her feet quickly and was in hot pursuit. The guineas ran as fast as their little legs would carry them but *Cocinera* was gaining on them. She was crazed and shrieking! Straw stuck out of her hair and the strong smell of onion wafted from her body. Their only chance was to squeeze under the gate or pop through one of its cracks before she scooped them up.

Pablo shoved Eva and the other guineas through the gate before sliding underneath. Jack unfortunately took a moment to look back, slowing him down. *Cocinera* missed with her net but grabbed him with her hand. Jack struck at her fingers with his dagger, while Pablo grasped Jack's other arm and pulled with such strength that *Cocinera* lost her grip and Jack popped through into the garden.

"*Les voy a chapar!*" yelled *Cocinera*.

She was moving so fast to open the gate and chase the guineas that when it didn't budge, her body hurled over and she landed on her head. Eva's idea to have the guineas block the gate probably saved their lives. Jack heard *Cocinera* yell out that she was going to catch them. This time, he didn't look back.

CHAPTER 11

Treasure

BT lifted Jack from his new cage and put him on his shoulder. Jack wiggled and snuggled in close. Jack had never felt this safe. Hours before returning to *Abuela's*, Pablo honored Jack in the hut after the rescue by making him an official member of the Wild Pack.

Jack was so exhausted when the Wild Pack finally got him back to *Abuela's* house that he slept for an entire day, not even waking to eat. When BT found Jack back inside his cage, he cried. Jack felt afraid when his human cried.

BT was so big and strong. Jack's heart fluttered. Time spent with the Wild Pack taught Jack that he wasn't "just a pet" but a responsible member of his own pack. BT needed Jack, Jack needed BT and they both needed Mother.

He thought about Pablo and how he cared for his children. Eva would suffer terribly if *Cocinera* cooked him. BT and Father must have had a special relationship too. BT's eyes were often swollen and red when Jack first met him. Jack vowed to himself he would be more careful and active to keep his pack safe. Jack wondered what he would do if something bad happened to BT - a single tear dropped to his paw. He was home, where he belonged.

Jack's belly rumbled. He immediately looked to BT's sockless foot and crawled down for his snack. It was bedtime, after all. Jack sniffed the crust for a moment trying to place the aroma. It was something new. He would just have to try it. He nibbled and found at first he didn't like it but with the second and third nibbles found it yummy. It was spicy and tasted like lemon.

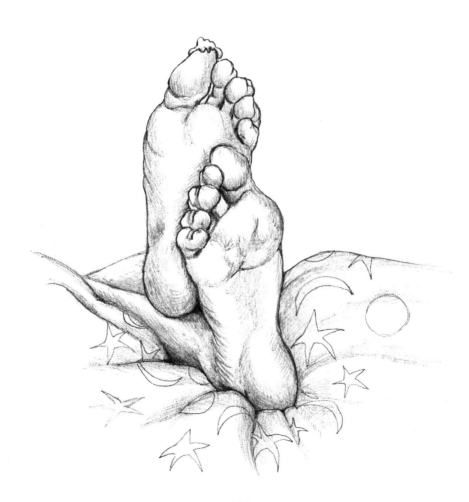

Jack looked up from his snack when he heard a familiar voice. Mother was coming.

"How's our little Jack?"

"He's back to his old self." BT smiled from ear to ear.

"What did you think of the *ceviche* for *almuerzo*?"

"It was pretty good for raw fish," said BT.

Oh, so that's what it was. They never ate that back in Knoxville.

"*Abuela* said we were supposed to have *cuy frito* for lunch but *Cocinera* fell and hit her head. She had to get ten stitches."

"Is *Abuela* crazy? I'm not eating guinea pig! That's like eating Jack! Mom, you have to talk to her!" BT's body tensed like a guitar string about to snap. He pleaded with Mother. Jack followed the conversation closely. It really was life or death for every guinea pig on the farm. Mother said not to worry, that she would speak with *Abuela*.

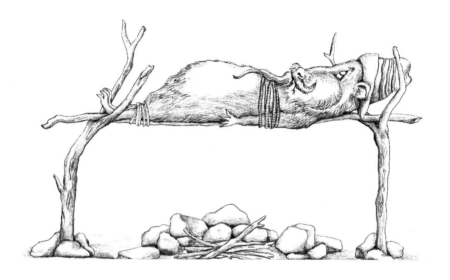

Jack tried to convince himself that while they were visiting *Abuela* the Wild Pack would be safe, but would they? Jack's plan to rescue Pablo and the others was such a success, maybe he should come up with another plan to protect the Wild Pack from his end of the farm.

BT calmed down, so Jack went back to his snack. He nibbled until the crust was gone then licked the spot of all traces of *ceviche*. Delicious! Jack didn't even mind that Mother messed up his mohawk. Wait a minute! Jack reached up and felt that his mohawk was unusually flat and messy. He hadn't sharpened it before he took charge of the big rescue? Well, that was strange, he thought but he was too tired to think anymore.

BT fluffed Jack's little blanket. "Jack, what's this?" BT pulled out the good luck charm Eva gave Jack after the big rescue. He held it up to the light and cleaned off the dirt with his t-shirt.

"Jack Attack! You did it! You found Incan Gold!"

Jack squealed with delight. BT danced around the room holding the gold coin in the air, then ran downstairs to show *Abuela* and Mother.

Jack looked to the doorway and smiled. The floor was clear. Jack had pushed two small bouncy balls to a corner so BT wouldn't slip when he came in and out of their room. Jack felt proud of himself. Just because he was the smallest member of his pack didn't mean he couldn't help.

He thought back to the night before the trip when Mother hurt her foot on the blocks. Jack decided to make it his job to keep their bedroom floor clean when they returned to Knoxville. Would BT even notice? It didn't matter.

"Pablo wasn't the only one who could protect his pack." Jack whispered then fell fast asleep with a smile on his face.

Spanish-English Word Glossary

Comida: Food

ají: spicy pepper

ajo: garlic

apio: celery

brocolí: brocoli

ceviche: ceviche (Peruvian dish of raw fish in lemon juice)

champiñon: mushroom

cuy frito: fried guinea pig

ensalada: salad

espárragos: asparagus

jugoso: juicy

lechuga: lettuce

maíz: corn

pepino: cucumber

perejíl: parsley

pimiento: bell pepper

tomate: tomato

trucha frita: fried trout

zanahoria: carrot

desayuno: breakfast

almuerzo: lunch

cena: dinner

Personajes: Characters

Abuela: grandmother

Cocinera: cook

Cuy: guinea pig

Profesor: teacher

Hijito: sweet son (in this book refers to grandson)

Otras: Others

comedor: dining room

escuela: school

flores: flowers

hacienda: ranch

montañas: mountains

Dichos: Phrases

Buenos días hijito: Good morning sweet son.

Que lindo cuy: What a sweet guinea pig.

Oye Benjamín, ven aquí un momentito: Hey Benjamin, come here for a moment.

Ven aquí: Come here.

Cuy rico y jugoso: Tasty and juicy guinea pig.

¡Te chapé!: I caught you!

¡Les voy a chapar!: I am going to catch you all!

Label the Vegetables in Spanish

ANDEAN CUSTOMS

CUY: In the Andes Mountain Range, which runs the length of South America, people raise guinea pigs for food. Guinea pig meat tastes very similar to chicken. The next time you're in Peru and don't know what to order in a restaurant, ask for *cuy frito*, fried guinea pig. *Delicioso!*

TERRACING: Where the mountains are steep, farmers dig large steps down the side of the mountain. Each step is made large enough to plant a crop. It's a beautiful site to see. *Maravilloso!*

ALMUERZO: Lunch is served at 3:00 approximately. It's the largest meal of the day. *Buen Apetito!*

WHO KNEW?

Peru is along the "Ring of Fire" which means there are many earthquakes. This frequent movement of the Earth's crust forces the mountains upward which will make the Andes Mountains the tallest in the world one day.

Who knew that mountains grew!